Miss You Like Crazy

by Pamela Hall

illustrated by Jennifer A. Bell

Tanglewood • Terre Haute, IN

For my children Adam, Emily and Jack. - PH

Text © 2014 Pamela Hall
Illustrations © 2014 Jennifer A. Bell

Design by Amy Alick Perich

Tanglewood Publishing, Inc.
4400 Hulman St.
Terre Haute, IN 47803
www.tanglewoodbooks.com

Printed in U.S.A.
10 9 8 7 6 5 4 3 2 1

ISBN 978-1-933718-91-0

Library of Congress Cataloging-in-Publication Data

Hall, Pamela, 1961-
  Miss you like crazy / by Pamela Hall ; illustrated by Jennifer A. Bell.
    pages cm
  Summary: Walnut does not want his mother to go to work without him, but after imagining the adventures they could share if he went along, she reassures him that he is always on her mind and plans to share special time with him each day.
  ISBN 978-1-933718-91-0 (hardback)
  [1. Mother and child--Fiction. 2. Squirrels--Fiction.] I. Bell, Jennifer (Jennifer A.), 1977- illustrator. II. Title.
  PZ7.H147513Mis 2014
  [Fic]--dc23
                    2013038081

Walnut crunched Honey Bumbles for breakfast.

"Ready to make tracks?" Mom asked.

"I want to stay home," Walnut groaned.
"Don't you miss me all day?"

"Only like crazy," Mom said,
snitching a Bumble crumb.

"I wish I could fold you up and pack you in my briefcase."

Walnut slipped into a
side pocket and hid.

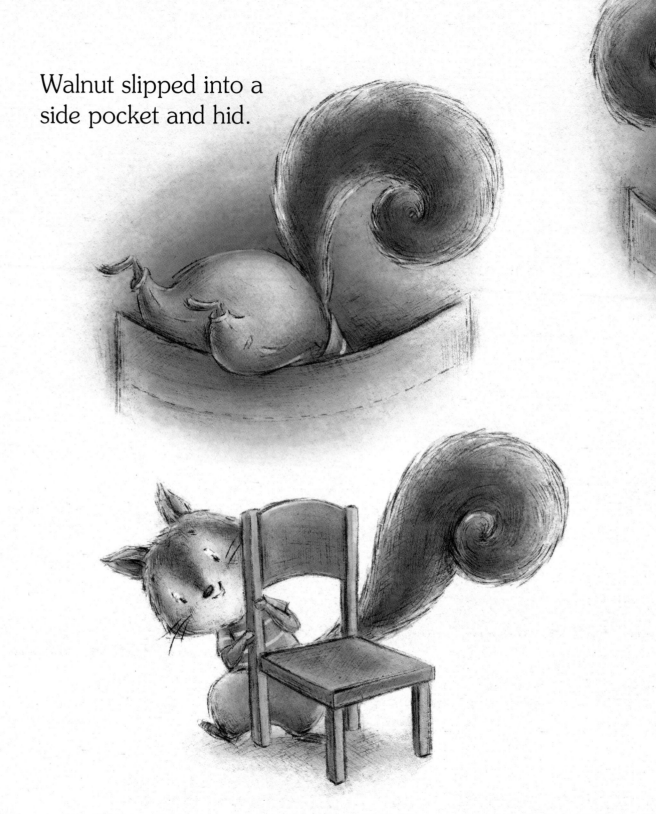

"I would pop out and scare you . . . BOO!"
Walnut shouted, springing from the pocket.

Mom snatched Walnut, twitching tail and all.
"Gotcha!" she said. "Captured in my pencil cup."

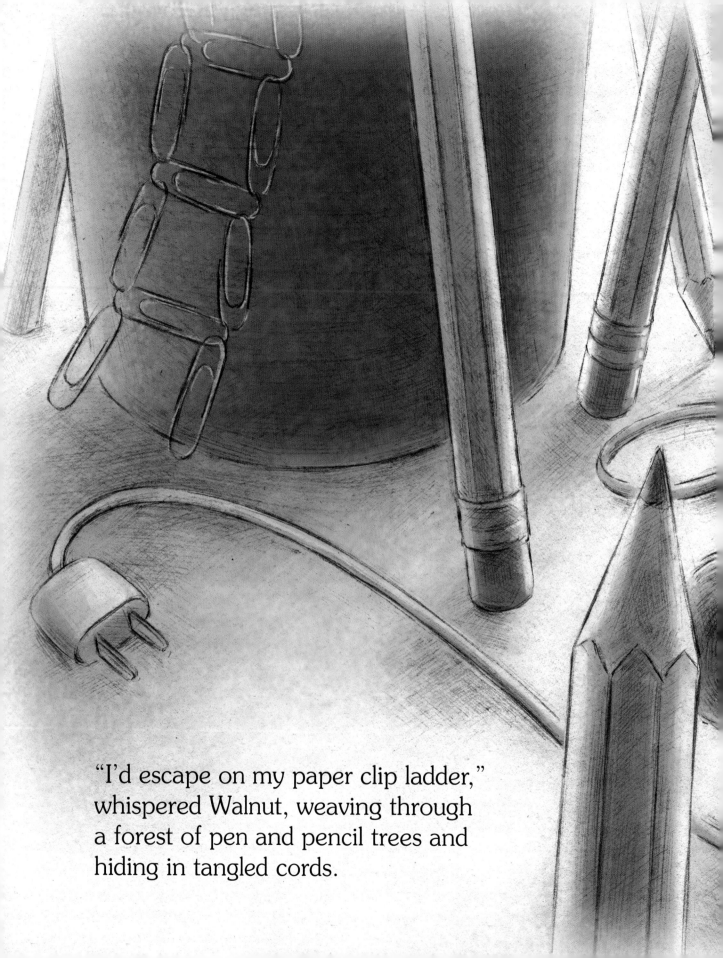

"I'd escape on my paper clip ladder," whispered Walnut, weaving through a forest of pen and pencil trees and hiding in tangled cords.

"But I would sniff you out and make you my mouse," said Mom.

"We'd scroll around the world, me and my laptop pilot."

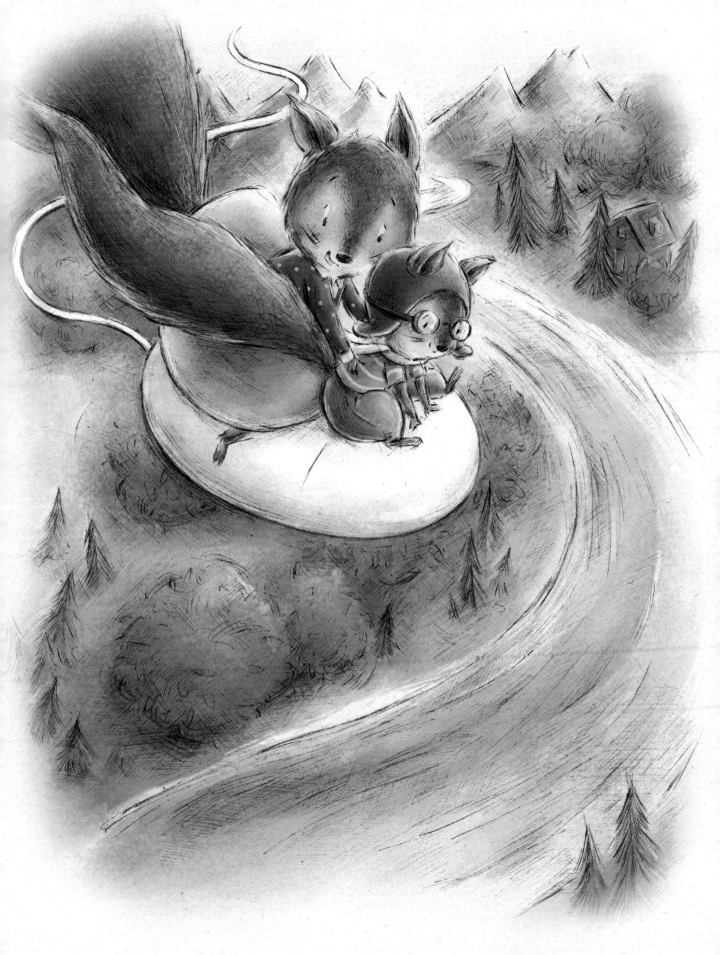

Walnut clicked on "Adventure" and donned a crown of gold and a long, velvet robe.

ADVENTURE

"I would be ruler of the jungle, and we'd swing with monkeys," Walnut declared.

"Then we would sail the seven seas and make friends with a whale," said Mom. "She would take us for a ride on her spout."

"To the beach!" Walnut shouted. "By then I would need something to eat!"

"I would buy us lunch at The Nut Hut," Mom said. "You would be the toy that comes with my meal. Then I would wear my Walnut shell necklace back to work."

"You'd have to go back?" Walnut asked.

"Yes," Mom said. "There are things I would need to do. People depend on me."

"For what?" Walnut wondered.

"I'll show you sometime—on Bring Your Child to Work Day," Mom promised. "But for now I proclaim each day at 5:00 to be Walnut Time."

Walnut smiled—5:00 would rock!

"But how come you have to work at all?" asked Walnut.

"Well," Mom explained, "I go to work so I can pay rent on our den and buy you Nutty Clusters and Super Squirrel socks. And I'm good at what I do."

"Just like you are good at
kickball and drawing."

Walnut considered this.

"But the best part of each day is
coming home to you," added Mom.

"I wish it was 5:00 now," Walnut
said. "Can we snuggle?"

Mom looked at her watch and then
relaxed, swallowing up Walnut in
her lap. "You bet—I love having you
close." Walnut curled into a ball of fur.

"I wish we could really stay together today. What if you get lonely without me?" Walnut asked, looking worried.

"But I am never really without you," Mom said.

"You're on my computer . . ."

"in my briefcase . . ."

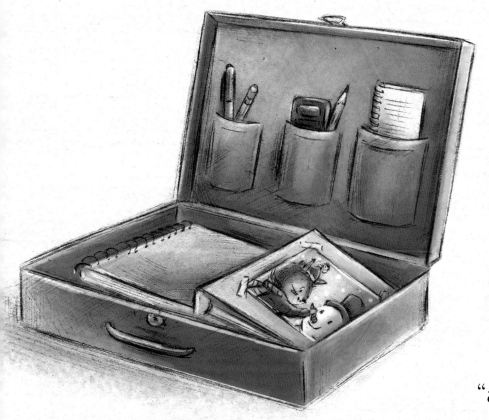

"at my desk . . ."

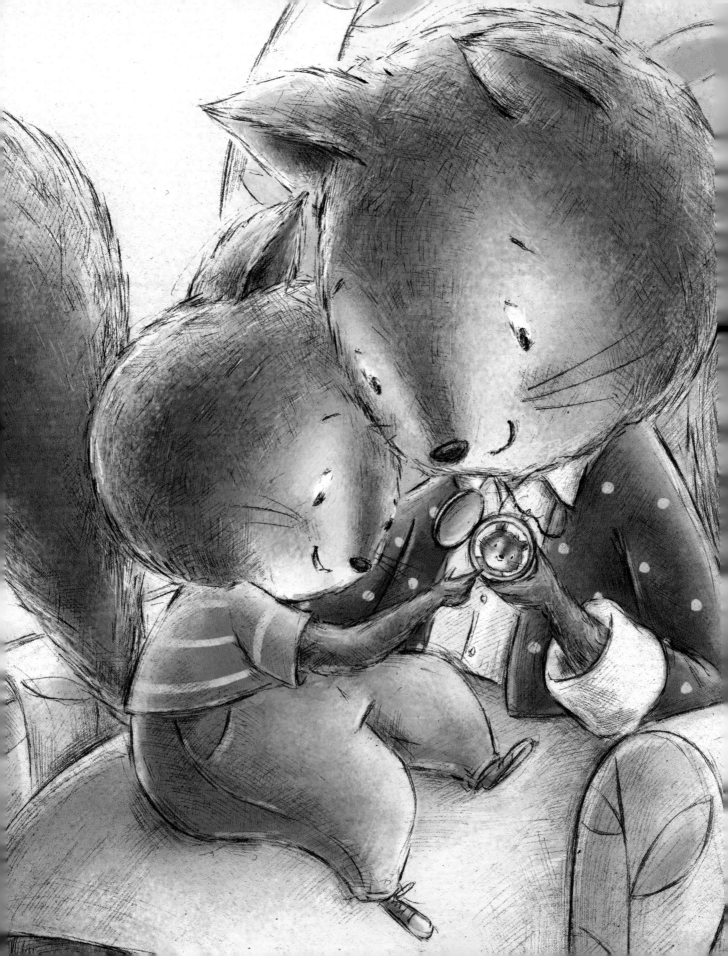

". . . around my neck
and on my mind."

"Everyone at work knows
you are my top priority."

"Mama, I miss you like crazy, too," Walnut said,
whisker to whisker with Mom. "Can I have a little
piece of you to keep with me all day?"

Mom smiled and said, "I think we can manage that."